The Lurking Fear

A Classic Lovecraftian Horror Story – Madness and Monstrosities

A Modern Translation

Adapted for the Contemporary Reader

H.P. Lovecraft

Translated by Tim Zengerink

Table of Contents

Preface - Message to the Reader

What If You Could Help Rebuild the Greatest Library in Human History?

Thousands of years ago, the Library of Alexandria stood as the crown jewel of human achievement — a sanctuary where the collected wisdom of every known civilization was gathered, preserved, and shared freely.

And then, it was lost.

Through fire, conquest, and the slow erosion of time, humanity lost not just books — but ideas, dreams, discoveries, and stories that could have changed the world forever.

Today, the Library of Alexandria lives again — and you are invited to be a part of its restoration.

Our mission is simple yet profound:

To rebuild the greatest library the world has ever known, and to translate all timeless works into every language and dialect, so that no seeker of knowledge is ever left behind again.

By joining our movement to rebuild the modern Library of Alexandria, you become part of an unprecedented mission:

- **Unlimited Access to the Greatest Audiobooks & eBooks Ever Written:**

  Instantly explore thousands of legendary works—Plato, Shakespeare, Jane Austen, Leo Tolstoy, and countless more. All instantly available to read or listen, placing a complete literary universe at your fingertips.

- **Beautiful Paperback & Deluxe Editions at Printing Cost**

  Own any title as an elegant paperback, deluxe hardcover, or stunning collectible boxset—offered to you at true printing cost, delivered straight to your door. Build your personal Library of Alexandria, crafted for beauty, built for durability, and worthy of proud display.

- **Fresh Translations for Modern Readers—in Every Language & Dialect**

  Enjoy timeless masterpieces reimagined in clear, contemporary language—no more outdated phrases or obscure references. Alongside the original versions, we're tirelessly translating these classics into every language and dialect imaginable, ensuring accessibility and understanding across cultures and generations.

- **Join a Global Renaissance of Literature & Knowledge**

  You directly support expanding our library, publishing deluxe editions at true cost, translating works into all global languages, and bringing humanity's greatest stories to people everywhere. By joining today, you're not just preserving a legacy of masterpieces; you set in motion a powerful wave of literary accessibility.

Become a Torchbearer of Knowledge.

Join us for free now at **LibraryofAlexandria.com**

Together, we will ensure that the light of human wisdom never fades again.

With gratitude and a shared love of knowledge,

The Modern Library of Alexandria Team

Visit:

www.libraryofalexandria.com

Or scan the code below:

Introduction

Degeneration, Ancestry, and the Monstrous Within

H.P. Lovecraft's "The Lurking Fear," originally serialized in Home Brew magazine in 1923, may not be as celebrated as his more iconic works like "The Call of Cthulhu" or "At the Mountains of Madness," but it remains one of the most atmospheric, fast-paced, and brutal entries in his extensive catalogue of horror. It serves as a bridge between his early pulp fiction and his later, more philosophically complex tales. The story brings together some of Lovecraft's most persistent themes—degeneracy, isolation, ancestral sin, and the thin boundary between civilization and savagery—while delivering a tale structured more like a horror serial than a cosmic meditation.

At its core, "The Lurking Fear" is an exploration of what lies beneath—both literally, in terms of physical descent into the earth, and metaphorically, in the descent into repressed human history, genetic degradation, and psychological fear. The unnamed narrator, a professional investigator of the bizarre and supernatural, ventures into the Catskill Mountains to investigate a series of grisly deaths attributed to strange, violent forces. He arrives at the storm-wracked Martense mansion, an ancient Dutch colonial estate whose aristocratic line has long since disappeared from civilized memory, and finds that the surrounding countryside lives in dread of the mansion and the land it commands.

The investigation quickly spirals into a series of nightmarish encounters with deformed creatures that seem to emerge from beneath the earth itself. Each expedition reveals more horror: whole communities of monstrous, ape-like beings, dead bodies torn apart, and underground networks of tunnels that stretch beneath the land like diseased veins. The horror culminates in the revelation that the Martense family, isolated for generations, had degenerated physically and mentally, eventually becoming the cannibalistic, subterranean monsters now haunting the hills.

This theme—the grotesque legacy of aristocratic bloodlines degraded by isolation and inbreeding—is common in Gothic literature, but Lovecraft injects it with his own twist. The fear is not just of the monstrous other, but of what that other reveals about humanity itself. The Martenses were once men, cultured and noble. Over time, cut off from society and civilization, they regressed into primal beasts. In this, Lovecraft articulates one of his most unsettling ideas: that monstrosity is not imposed from without, but lies dormant within. Civilization, in this worldview, is a fragile mask—one that can slip or rot, revealing the bestial truths we strive to deny.

The Gothic Lineage and the Anatomy of Fear

Lovecraft's choice to set the tale in the remote Catskills is more than scenic—it ties directly into his American Gothic inheritance. While classic European Gothic literature often placed its horrors in ancient castles and Old World ruins, Lovecraft transplanted these anxieties into the backwoods and decaying estates of New England and rural America. "The Lurking Fear" is one of his clearest nods to this transformation. The Martense mansion, with its Dutch ancestry, rotting timbers, and thunder-blasted silhouette, is a quintessential American equivalent of the haunted castle. It represents not just architectural decay, but the moral and biological rot that festers in isolation.

The narrator's voice is intense, urgent, and increasingly frayed as the story progresses. There is no long philosophical buildup here as in "The Shadow Out of Time" or "The Whisperer in Darkness." This is Lovecraft in his most kinetic form—more in line with pulp horror than metaphysical dread. Each chapter is structured to deliver new revelations and ever-escalating fear. Lightning flashes, bodies are mutilated, and monstrous eyes gleam in the dark. The pacing is relentless, and the imagery brutal.

Yet beneath the pulp stylings lies a much deeper fear—of regression, of devolution, of the body and mind surrendering to animalistic instinct. Lovecraft was deeply influenced by both Darwinian theory and early 20th-century concerns about eugenics and atavism. In "The Lurking Fear," this influence is clear. The Martenses are not supernatural creatures. They are the result of biology, of human potential corrupted by isolation, bad breeding, and environmental pressure. Their transformation is horrifying not because it is unnatural, but because it is plausible.

This realism is part of what makes the story effective. Unlike many of Lovecraft's tales that feature alien gods and ancient tomes, this one takes place entirely within the boundaries of Earth, human history, and scientific possibility. There are no Necronomicons, no cosmic entities, no vast mythologies—only men turned monstrous by the slow grinding of time, hunger, and darkness.

The final revelation—that the narrator himself has seen the Martense patriarch in the form of a monstrous being whose eyes echo the family's old portrait—drives home the horror of recognition. The line between human and inhuman is not as firm as we would like to think. That which lurks is not always foreign. Sometimes, it is our own past, our own blood, our own reflection—distorted but still recognizable.

Influence, Interpretation, and the Legacy of a Lesser-Known Masterwork

While "The Lurking Fear" is often overshadowed by Lovecraft's more mythos-heavy stories, it has played a quict but important role in shaping the genre of American horror fiction. Its influence can be seen in the works of Stephen King, especially in Pet Sematary and Jerusalem's Lot, both of which explore decaying rural landscapes, ancestral evil, and buried monstrosities. The trope of the degenerate family living in isolation—a fixture of modern horror from The Texas Chain Saw Massacre to The Hills Have Eyes—owes much to Lovecraft's Martense clan.

Furthermore, the story serves as a prototype for Lovecraft's evolving style. Here, we see the transition from overt Gothic horror to psychological and biological terror. It lacks the cosmic scope of his later work, but it contains all the seeds: the dread of ancestry, the unreliability of perception, the horror of buried knowledge, and the collapse of rational boundaries in the face of ancient truth.

"The Lurking Fear" also stands out for its unrelenting physicality. Lovecraft's horror is often cerebral and atmospheric, but in this story, the violence is graphic and the monstrosities are tangible. He uses texture, smell, and sound to make the horror visceral: the reek of decay, the crunch of bones, the suffocating darkness of tunnels. This grounding in the body—the fear of what happens when flesh forgets its form—is rare in Lovecraft, and makes this tale especially immediate.

This modern edition has been carefully updated for clarity and accessibility. While the narrative voice and stylistic intensity remain intact, archaic phrases have been refined and over-complicated structures streamlined. The goal is to allow modern readers to experience the story's dread, pacing, and psychological weight without linguistic interference. The horror is Lovecraft's; the path to it has been cleared for a contemporary journey.

Reading "The Lurking Fear" today is to confront a question that echoes throughout all of Lovecraft's work: What happens when the boundaries between past and present, between man and monster, begin to dissolve? It is to explore the fear that beneath the floorboards of civilization—beneath memory, culture, and rational thought—lurks something older, hungrier, and less human than we care to admit.

This edition invites you into the storm, to the rotting walls of the Martense mansion, to the tunnels beneath the mountains. It asks you to look into the dark and ask not what lies waiting—but whether it recognizes you. And when you feel it looking back, when its eyes mirror your own, you will understand what Lovecraft meant by the lurking fear—not a beast in the forest, but the beast in the blood.

Chapter 1
The Shadow on the Chimney

There was a storm in the air the night I went to the abandoned mansion on Tempest Mountain to uncover the lurking fear. I wasn't alone—my curiosity for strange and scary things had never made me reckless. I had brought two strong, reliable men who had helped me before on other eerie investigations. They were used to these kinds of unsettling journeys and knew how to handle themselves.

We left the village quietly, trying to avoid the reporters still hanging around after last month's terrifying event—the so-called creeping death that spread panic through the area. I thought I might need the reporters later, but not that night. Looking back, I wish I had let them come along. Maybe then I wouldn't have had to keep this awful secret by myself for so long. I stayed quiet because I feared people would think I was crazy—or worse, lose their minds over what I had discovered. But now I have to tell it, before the memory drives me mad. I alone know what kind of horror waited on that haunted, empty mountain.

We drove through miles of old forest and rolling hills in a small car until the steep slope forced us to continue on foot. The land felt unusually creepy under the dark sky, especially without the usual crowd of investigators around. More than once, we considered turning on the headlights, even though we didn't want to attract attention. The woods didn't feel right after dark. Even if I hadn't known about the terror hiding there, I think I still would've sensed something was wrong. We saw no animals—they knew better than to stay near death. The lightning-damaged trees looked weirdly huge and twisted, and the thick plants seemed sick and wild. The bumpy ground was covered in strange shapes that reminded me of snakes or huge, swollen skulls.

Fear had haunted Tempest Mountain for over a hundred years. I first learned this from news reports about the disaster that had made people notice the area. The mountain is a remote, lonely spot in the Catskills, where Dutch settlers once lived for a short time. When they left, only a few ruined houses and poor squatter families remained, living in run-down huts on the hills. Regular people rarely visited, even after the state police started patrolling. Still, the nearby villages had always spoken about the fear. It was a common story among the ragged locals who sometimes came out of the hills to trade their handmade baskets for food and supplies they couldn't hunt or grow.

The fear was tied to the abandoned Martense mansion, which sat at the top of a tall hill that often got hit by lightning, earning it the name Tempest Mountain. For over a century, that old stone house had been at the center of horrifying tales—stories of a silent, creeping death that roamed the area during summer. The squatters whispered about a demon that grabbed people walking alone at night, either taking them or leaving their bodies horribly torn apart. They even claimed to find trails of blood leading toward the mansion. Some said the thunder called the creature out, while others believed the thunder was its voice.

Most people outside the backwoods didn't believe these confusing, over-the-top stories. The creature was always only half-seen, and the descriptions never made much sense. Still, no one nearby doubted the mansion was haunted. The local history was enough to keep that fear alive, even though investigators never found ghosts when they searched the building after one of the more intense stories spread. Elders told strange stories about the Martense family—about their odd, mismatched eyes, their strange past, and a murder that had cursed their name.

The event that finally brought me there was a shocking confirmation of the wildest local tales. One summer night, after a storm more violent than any before, a wave of terror swept through the hills. Squatters fled in a panic no ordinary fear could cause. They wailed about a horror too awful to name. They hadn't seen it—but the screams they'd heard from one of their villages told them that something had come in the night. Something that killed without being seen.

The thunder rolled through the sky the morning after the attack, as local people and state troopers followed the terrified mountaineers to the spot where they said death had struck. And it had. The ground beneath one of the squatters' villages had collapsed after being hit by lightning, destroying several filthy shacks. But worse than the property damage was the horror left behind. Of the seventy-five people who lived there, not one was found alive. The broken earth was soaked in blood and littered with human remains—clear signs of a brutal attack by something with sharp teeth and claws. But strangely, there were no tracks showing where the creature had come from or gone.

Everyone agreed some kind of terrifying animal must have done it. No one claimed anymore that it was just another crime in a rough community. That theory returned only when they realized about twenty-five people were missing from the scene, but even then, it didn't explain how so few could've killed so many. All that could be confirmed was that a lightning storm hit one summer night—and when it passed, it left behind a dead village, filled with bodies horribly torn apart.

People quickly connected this horror to the old, abandoned Martense mansion, even though it was more than three miles away. The state police weren't convinced. They checked the house quickly and dismissed it when they found it completely empty. But the local villagers searched every inch. They went through the house, checked the ponds and creeks, beat through the bushes, and combed the nearby woods. Still, they found nothing. Whatever had caused the death had vanished without a trace—leaving only destruction behind.

By the second day, the newspapers picked up the story. Reporters flooded Tempest Mountain, writing detailed articles and interviewing locals who shared old tales. At first, I only followed their stories half-heartedly. I've always had a strong interest in horrors, but something about this one began to disturb me in a way I couldn't explain. So on August 5th, 1921, I joined the reporters in Lefferts Corners—the nearest village and the base for all the search efforts. Three weeks later, when the reporters left, I finally had the chance to begin my own intense investigation. I had spent that time asking questions and studying the area, preparing for what I now knew I had to do.

That's how, on a summer night with thunder rumbling in the distance, I left my silent car and hiked up the hills of Tempest Mountain with two armed companions. We used our flashlights to light the path as the huge, ghostly stone walls of the mansion came into view between the twisted trees. The place looked even scarier at night than it did during the day. But I didn't hesitate. I had a strong feeling that the thunder somehow called the creature from its hidden lair—and whether it was a real monster or some kind of deadly sickness, I was determined to see it for myself.

I had already explored the ruins thoroughly, so I knew exactly where to go. I chose the old room of Jan Martense for our watch. He was the murder victim mentioned often in the local legends, and I felt this room was the right place for our plan. It was about twenty feet square, on the second floor, in the southeast corner. There were two windows—one large and one small—both without glass or shutters. Across from the large window was a massive fireplace decorated with tile scenes from the Bible, and across from the smaller window was a built-in wall bed.

As the thunder got louder, I set up our plan. I tied three rope ladders to the big window so we could escape outside if needed. I had tested them before and knew they reached the ground. Then, we moved a large bed from another room and pushed it up against the window. We covered it with pine branches and all lay down with guns ready. We took turns resting and watching. If the monster came from inside, we'd escape through the window. If it came from outside, we'd use the door. Based on past stories, we didn't think it would chase us very far.

My watch lasted from midnight to 1 a.m. Even with the creepy mansion, open window, and approaching storm, I began to feel sleepy. I lay between my two companions—George Bennett by the window and William Tobey near the fireplace. Bennett had already fallen asleep, likely feeling the same strange drowsiness I did. I assigned Tobey to take the next watch, though he was clearly struggling to stay awake too. I couldn't stop staring at the fireplace.

The growing thunder must have affected my dreams, because in the short time I slept, I had terrifying visions. I half-woke once when Bennett's arm flopped across my chest, but I wasn't fully awake. I didn't know if Tobey was still watching, but something didn't feel right. I had never felt such a deep sense of evil. I must have fallen asleep again, because I was suddenly jolted awake by horrifying screams—worse than anything I'd ever heard or imagined.

Those screams were full of terror and pain, like a soul being torn apart. I woke up in a rush of panic and confusion. The room was pitch black. I could tell Tobey was gone—only an empty space remained where he had been. But Bennett's heavy arm still lay across my chest.

Then a huge bolt of lightning hit, shaking the whole mountain. It lit up the darkest parts of the forest and split the oldest, most twisted tree. In that terrifying flash, the person sleeping next to me suddenly sat up. The light from outside threw his shadow onto the chimney above the fireplace—the same spot I had been watching the entire time.

It's honestly a miracle I'm still alive and not completely insane. I don't understand how, because the shadow I saw on the chimney wasn't George Bennett's—or any human's. It was something terrifying, something straight out of a nightmare. It didn't have a clear shape, and it was so unnatural that it's impossible to describe. No one could truly understand what it was.

A moment later, I was completely alone in that haunted house, trembling and talking to myself. George Bennett and William Tobey were gone—without a single clue left behind. No signs of a fight, nothing. They were never seen again.

Chapter 2
A Passer in the Storm

For days after that terrifying experience in the forest-covered mansion, I stayed in my hotel room at Lefferts Corners, completely drained and on edge. I can't remember clearly how I got back to the car, started it, and made my way back to town without being seen. All I can recall are giant trees waving wildly, thunder rumbling like something alive, and strange shadows creeping across the bumpy ground.

As I sat there, shaken and thinking about the horrifying shadow I'd seen, I realized I had come face to face with something beyond anything on Earth. It was one of those unknown terrors from the edge of space—things we're usually lucky enough not to see. I didn't want to figure out what that shadow had really been. Something had stood between me and the window that night, but I couldn't help trying to make sense of it. If it had just made a noise—growled or even laughed—that might have made it less terrifying. But it had been silent. And it had rested something heavy, like an arm or leg, on my chest. Whatever it was, it had once been alive. Jan Martense, whose room I'd been in, was buried in the nearby graveyard... I had to find out what happened to Bennett and Tobey. Why had it taken them and left me? I was slipping into sleep again, and the dreams were horrifying.

Eventually, I knew I had to tell someone what happened or I'd lose my mind. I wasn't ready to give up my search for the lurking fear. Not knowing felt worse than learning the awful truth. So I began thinking about who I could trust with this secret and who might help me uncover the thing that took two men and left behind a nightmare.

The reporters I'd met in Lefferts Corners were friendly, and some were still around gathering the last bits of news. After some thought, I chose Arthur Munroe to help me. He was a quiet, serious man around thirty-five, smart and open-minded—someone who wasn't scared off by strange ideas.

One September afternoon, I told Arthur everything. He listened closely and understood the situation right away. He gave solid advice, suggesting we wait to go back to the mansion until we had more history and background about the place. At his suggestion, we explored the countryside, learning more about the twisted history of the Martense family. We found one man with an old family diary full of important details.

We also talked to some of the squatters who hadn't run away and made plans to fully explore both the mansion and the areas tied to past stories of terror.

At first, these efforts didn't give us much. But after organizing the information, we noticed a pattern: most of the horror reports came from areas near the mansion or connected to it through thick, unhealthy-looking forest. Some reports were exceptions, though—like the one that caught the world's attention, which happened in a treeless field far from the mansion or any woods.

We couldn't learn much about the creature itself from the frightened squatters. They described it in so many different ways—it was a snake, a giant, a demon, a bat, a walking tree. Despite the confusion, we believed it was a real creature that reacted strongly to lightning storms. Some stories made it sound like it had wings, but we figured it mostly moved on the ground. The only thing that didn't fit was how fast it would have to move to do all the things people said it did.

As we got to know the squatters better, we found them strangely likable. They were simple people, slowly regressing due to isolation and poor ancestry. Though they feared outsiders, they began to warm up to us and helped when we tore through the house, pulling apart walls and bushes to find the lurking fear. They truly wanted to help us find Bennett and Tobey, even though they were certain the two men had vanished just like many of their own.

By mid-October, we were frustrated. Clear skies had kept the monster quiet, and we had found nothing in our searches. We began to wonder if it was some kind of ghost or invisible force. Winter was coming, and we feared our search would soon have to end. So we pushed ourselves harder, returning to one of the abandoned hamlets during the day. The place was now empty, thanks to the squatters' fear.

The village had no name. It sat in a bare valley between two hills—Cone Mountain and Maple Hill. It was closer to Maple Hill, with some homes dug into the hillside. It was about two miles northwest of the base of Tempest Mountain, and three miles from the Martense mansion. Between the village and the mansion was mostly open land—flat, with only grass and weeds growing. Because of this, we guessed the creature had come from Cone Mountain, where the forest stretched closest to the mansion. The caved-in ground matched a landslide from Maple Hill, right where a tall, broken tree stood—the one that had been struck by lightning the night the horror appeared.

***

As Arthur Munroe and I searched the ruined village for what felt like the twentieth time, we were starting to feel hopeless. It was strange—and unsettling—that after something so horrible had happened, we couldn't find a single clue. The sky above was dark and heavy, and we wandered through the empty ruins with a mix of frustration and urgency, driven by the need to do something even though we kept coming up empty. We searched everything again—each cabin, each dugout, every thorny slope nearby. Still, we found nothing. And yet, something felt wrong. A strange, creeping fear hung over us, like invisible monsters were watching us from the mountain tops.

As the afternoon wore on, the light faded fast, and thunder began to roll over Tempest Mountain. It made us uneasy, but not as much as it would have if it were nighttime. Still, we hoped the storm would last until dark, thinking it might somehow help us find answers. With that in mind, we stopped our search and headed for a nearby village to ask some of the younger squatters to help us. A few of them, encouraged by our leadership, agreed to come along.

But before we could go far, a sudden downpour slammed down on us. The rain was so heavy and the sky so dark it felt like night had fallen early. We stumbled around for a bit but managed to reach the sturdiest cabin, one we knew well from our many searches. It was a patched-together shelter made of logs and boards, with one small window and a door facing Maple Hill. We shut the door against the wind and rain, secured the window shutter, and sat down on some old crates in the pitch-black room. It was gloomy, but we lit our pocket flashlights now and then and smoked our pipes as we waited. The lightning outside lit up the cracks in the walls, and because the storm had made the day so dark, every flash was bright and sharp.

Sitting there, the storm made me think of my awful night on Tempest Mountain. One question kept coming back to me—why had the creature attacked the men on either side of me and left me for last? Did it plan to do something worse to me? Why hadn't it followed a simple pattern, no matter which direction it came from? What kind of creature could do such a thing? Or had it known I was the leader and saved me for something worse?

Just as these thoughts ran through my mind, a huge bolt of lightning struck nearby, followed by the sound of earth sliding. At the same time, the wind howled louder than ever. We figured the tall tree on Maple Hill had been struck again. Munroe stood up and went to the window to see what had happened. When he opened the shutter, wind and rain blasted into the room so loudly I couldn't hear what he said. I stayed seated while he leaned out, trying to see through the chaos outside.

Eventually, the wind began to die down, and the strange darkness faded. I had hoped the storm would last longer to help us in our search, but a thin ray of sunlight slipping in through a crack in the wall made it clear that wasn't going to happen. I told Munroe we should get some light and opened the cabin door. Outside, the ground was muddy and full of puddles, with fresh piles of dirt from the small landslide—but nothing seemed worth staring at.

Still, Munroe hadn't moved from the window. Curious, I went over and touched his shoulder. He didn't react. I gave him a little shake and turned him around—and that's when I was hit with a wave of horror so deep it felt like it came from the beginning of time itself.

Arthur Munroe was dead.

And whatever had killed him had chewed and torn at his head so badly that his face was completely gone.

Chapter 3
What the Red Glare Meant

On the stormy night of November 8th, 1921, I stood alone in a graveyard, digging up the grave of Jan Martense by lantern light. The shadows it cast looked like something out of a nightmare. I'd started digging earlier that day because I knew a thunderstorm was coming, and by the time it hit—pouring rain and rumbling through the thick trees—I was glad. The storm somehow matched the madness inside me.

I think my mind had started to break after everything that had happened since August 5th. The terrifying shadow in the mansion, the constant stress and failures, and especially what happened in that hamlet during the October storm—it all added up. After that horrible night, I buried someone whose death I couldn't explain. No one could. I let people believe Arthur Munroe had just wandered off. They searched but found nothing. The squatters might've known more, but I couldn't risk scaring them even more than they already were.

Something had changed in me after that night at the mansion. My mind felt numb, and all I could think about was solving the mystery—finding the source of this fear that had grown into something huge and overwhelming. Arthur's death only made me more determined, and I knew I had to do this on my own, without telling anyone.

The graveyard itself was terrifying enough. Massive, ancient trees loomed over me like twisted pillars in some nightmare forest. Their thick branches muffled the thunder and blocked most of the rain. In the distance, lit by faint lightning flashes, I could just make out the ruins of the old Martense mansion. Closer by was the abandoned Dutch garden, filled with sick-looking plants that never saw sunlight, and right next to me were the graves. Deformed trees swayed above broken tombstones, their roots pulling at the stones and feeding off whatever was buried beneath. Sometimes I could see the low, strange mounds that marked the graves, barely visible under the dead leaves and darkness.

It was history that had brought me here. After all the horror and confusion, history was the only thing I had left to rely on. I'd come to believe the lurking fear wasn't a real creature, but the ghost of Jan Martense—some wolf-like spirit riding the storms. Based on all the old stories I'd uncovered with Arthur, I was convinced

Jan's spirit still haunted the land. That's why I was digging up his grave, like some madman.

The Martense mansion had been built in 1670 by Gerrit Martense, a rich merchant from New Amsterdam. He didn't like the new British rule and wanted to live somewhere far away from it all. He picked a lonely hill in the woods for his fancy new home, drawn to its wild beauty. At first, he thought the frequent thunderstorms were just bad luck, but over time he realized the area got hit far more than normal. The storms began to bother him so much that he had a cellar built, just so he could hide from them during the worst ones.

Not much is known about Gerrit's descendants. They were raised to hate the British way of life and avoided people who didn't share their views. They lived in isolation and were known for being slow to speak and understand. They also had a strange inherited trait—one blue eye and one brown. Over time, they stopped connecting with the outside world entirely and started marrying into the servant class that worked on the estate. Many of them eventually left the mansion, moved across the valley, and became part of the mixed group of people who would later become the squatters. The few who stayed behind in the mansion became even more withdrawn, yet strangely sensitive to the frequent summer storms.

Most of what the outside world knew about the Martense family came from young Jan Martense. Unlike his relatives, Jan felt restless and ended up joining the colonial army after hearing about the Albany Convention. He was the first of Gerrit's descendants to truly see the world, and when he came back in 1760 after six years of service, his family no longer accepted him. Even though he still had the family's unique mismatched eyes, they saw him as an outsider. He couldn't relate to their strange ways anymore, and even the thunderstorms that used to thrill him now just made him feel low. He often wrote letters to a friend in Albany, saying he wanted to leave his family home.

In the spring of 1763, Jan's friend Jonathan Gifford became worried after not hearing from him for a while. Knowing the tensions in the Martense household, Gifford decided to visit Jan himself. He rode on horseback into the mountains and arrived at Tempest Mountain on September 20th. The mansion was falling apart, and the Martense family—sullen and with mismatched eyes—looked dirty and almost animal-like, which shocked Gifford. In broken, awkward speech, they told him Jan had died the fall before, supposedly struck by lightning. They showed him a grave behind the old, neglected gardens, but there was no marker on it. Their behavior seemed suspicious, and Gifford couldn't shake the feeling that something wasn't right. A week later, he came back with digging tools to check the grave himself. What he found confirmed his fears—a skull crushed by brutal blows. He returned to Albany and accused the Martenses of murdering Jan.

There wasn't enough legal proof to act on, but the story quickly spread. People stopped having anything to do with the Martense family, and their house became known as a cursed place. Still, they managed to live off their land, and from time to time, people saw lights coming from the mansion—even as late as 1810. But over time, the lights grew fewer and finally stopped.

As years passed, creepy stories about the mansion and mountain spread. People avoided the place even more, filling in the gaps with dark legends. The mansion remained untouched until 1816, when locals noticed the lights were gone. A group went to investigate and found the house empty and falling apart.

There were no bones or signs of death, so it seemed like the family had simply left. Makeshift shelters around the house suggested there had been many of them before they disappeared. The furniture was rotting, and silverware was left behind, showing how far the family had fallen before they left. Even though the Martenses were gone, fear of the house stayed strong—especially when new, strange stories began to come from the people still living in the mountains.

And that haunted house, tied forever to the vengeful ghost of Jan Martense, still stood in silence on the night I dug into his grave.

***

I've called my digging foolish, and it really was—both in why I did it and how I went about it. I found Jan Martense's coffin quickly, but it held only dust and bits of minerals. Still, in my obsession to dig up his ghost, I kept digging deeper, without thinking clearly. I don't even know what I expected to find. I only knew I was digging where someone's spirit was said to walk at night.

I have no idea how deep I went before my shovel—and then my feet—broke through the floor of the grave. It was a huge moment for me, because it seemed to prove my wild theory: something was hiding beneath the earth. When I fell, my lantern went out, but I had a small flashlight in my pocket. I turned it on and saw a low tunnel stretching out in both directions. It was just big enough for a person to crawl through. Anyone thinking clearly wouldn't have gone in—but I wasn't thinking clearly. I didn't care about the danger, or how filthy it was. I had only one goal: to find the lurking fear. So I chose the path that led toward the house and crawled in, dragging myself forward quickly, only turning on the light now and then.

How can I even explain what it was like? A man, lost deep underground, crawling and gasping, twisting through ancient darkness, without any idea where he was going or even why—just blindly pushing ahead. It was terrifying, but that's exactly what I did. I did it for so long that the world above seemed like a faint memory. I felt more like some underground creature than a man. Eventually, by pure chance, I bumped my flashlight in a way that made it flicker back on. It lit up the tight tunnel ahead of me with a pale, ghostly glow.

I kept crawling, but the battery was dying. Then the tunnel suddenly tilted upward, forcing me to climb instead of crawl. As I looked up, I saw something that made me freeze. In the distance, two glowing eyes reflected the dim light of my flashlight. The way they glowed made something stir deep in my memory, but I couldn't place it. I couldn't move—I just stared. The thing with those eyes crept closer, but I could only see a claw. And that claw was unlike anything I'd ever imagined.

Then I heard a faint crashing sound above. It was the thunder from the storm raging on the mountain—wild and violent. I realized I must be close to the surface again. But even as the thunder roared, the glowing eyes stared at me with a blank, awful look.

Thank God I didn't understand what I was looking at in that moment. If I had, I might've died from shock. But then the very storm that brought the creature also saved me. A massive lightning strike ripped through the ground above me. It was so loud and bright that it nearly knocked me out, but not completely.

As the earth shifted and collapsed around me, I clawed my way up blindly. The cold rain hitting my head brought me back to my senses, and I saw that I had reached the surface. I was on a steep, treeless slope on the mountain's southwest side. Flashes of lightning lit up the wrecked land around me, and I saw what remained of a strange mound that had stretched down from the forested slope above. But there was nothing left to show where I'd come from. My mind felt as scrambled as the ground, and when I noticed a red glow far off in the distance, I barely understood what I was seeing.

It wasn't until two days later, when the local squatters told me what the red glow meant, that true horror hit me. In a village twenty miles away, just after the same lightning bolt that freed me, something had fallen from a tree onto the roof of a fragile cabin. It did something terrible—so awful that the people set the cabin on fire in a panic before the creature could escape. That thing had been attacking at the exact same moment the ground had caved in on the creature I saw underground—the one with the claw and the glowing eyes. And that realization terrified me more than anything else.

Chapter 4
The Horror in the Eyes

No one in their right mind would go looking for the horror on Tempest Mountain after everything I had already seen. Even knowing that two of those terrifying creatures were gone didn't make it feel much safer. Still, I kept searching, more determined than ever as each new clue made the mystery even more disturbing.

Just two days after crawling through that awful underground tunnel with the eyes and the claw, I found out that a creature had been spotted twenty miles away—at the same time I'd seen those glowing eyes underground. That news terrified me so much I nearly passed out. But mixed with the fear was a strange kind of fascination, something so weird and surreal that it almost felt exciting. It reminded me of those nightmares where you're flying over creepy, dead cities and you feel strangely drawn to fall into the endless darkness. That's how it felt—like I wanted to dig deep into the cursed mountain and rip the evil out with my bare hands.

I went back to Jan Martense's grave as soon as I could and tried digging again. But a large cave-in had wiped out any sign of the tunnel I'd fallen into before, and rain had filled the hole so much that I couldn't tell how deep I'd gone last time.

I also made a tough trip to the distant village where the creature had attacked and been burned. I didn't find much there. In the ashes of the destroyed cabin, I saw a few bones, but none that looked like they belonged to the monster. The locals said the thing had only killed one person, but I didn't believe them. Besides the full skull of a person, there was also a bone that seemed like part of another human skull. Even though people saw it fall from a tree, no one could describe what it looked like. They just called it a devil. The tree it had been hiding in showed no strange marks, and I couldn't bring myself to go back into that creepy forest with its huge, twisted roots.

Next, I returned to the abandoned hamlet where the most deaths had happened—and where Arthur Munroe had seen something so horrifying it cost him his life. I had already searched this place very carefully before, but now I had a new idea. After crawling underground that night, I was convinced that at least one version of this creature lived below the surface. So on November 14th, I focused on the hillsides around the village, especially near Cone Mountain and Maple Hill, and the area where the landslide had happened.

That afternoon, I didn't find anything new. As the sun set, I stood on Maple Hill, looking down at the empty village and across the valley at Tempest Mountain. The sunset had been beautiful, and now the moon was nearly full, casting silver light across the field, the mountain, and the strange little mounds scattered around. It looked peaceful, like a postcard—but knowing what was buried there made me feel sick. I hated the way everything looked so calm and innocent. I hated the moon, the land, the mountain, and especially those strange mounds. It all felt infected by something rotten and evil.

As I stood there, lost in thought, something about the layout of the land caught my attention. Even though I wasn't a geologist, I had always thought those odd little hills were shaped strangely. They seemed to form lines that spread out from the top of Tempest Mountain. Now, with the long moon shadows, I saw it clearly—they looked like they were reaching out from the mountain, like some kind of tentacles made of earth. That image sent a chill through me. I started questioning my earlier belief that these were just natural hills made by glaciers.

The more I thought about it, the more it felt like something else. My memory flashed back to being underground and what I'd seen there. Suddenly I was muttering to myself in a panic: "Oh God… molehills… the place is full of tunnels… how many… that night at the mansion… they took Bennett and Tobey first… on either side…" Then I snapped and started digging wildly into the nearest mound. I was shaking but almost thrilled when I hit a tunnel—just like the one I'd crawled through on that horrible night.

After that, everything's a blur. I remember running with my shovel through moonlit fields and haunted woods, screaming and stumbling as I raced toward the Martense mansion. I dug all over the overgrown cellar, trying to find the heart of the evil that lived beneath the ground. Then, I laughed like a madman when I found it—an opening at the base of the old chimney, hidden by thick weeds, flickering in the light of the small candle I'd brought.

I had no idea what was still hiding in that nightmare den, waiting for the thunder to wake it up again. Maybe it was all over. Two of them were dead, maybe that was the end. But I couldn't stop now. I had to find out the truth—because now I believed, without a doubt, that the fear was real. It was something solid, something alive, and something hiding deep in the earth.

I wasn't sure whether I should explore the tunnel right away with just my flashlight, or wait and try to gather some of the local squatters to help me. But before I could decide, a sudden gust of wind rushed in from outside, blowing out my candle and leaving me in total darkness. The moonlight had disappeared too—no longer shining through the cracks and holes above. Then I heard a deep, threatening rumble of thunder in the distance, and a wave of fear rushed over me.

My thoughts were all over the place as I slowly made my way toward the farthest corner of the cellar, not knowing what else to do. Still, I couldn't look away from the dark opening at the base of the chimney. Every time lightning flashed through the trees outside, it lit up the gaps in the wall and gave me quick glimpses of the crumbling bricks and the sickly weeds growing around the entrance.

Fear and curiosity battled inside me with every passing second. What would the storm bring out this time—if anything was even left down there? When another flash of lightning lit the room, I crouched behind a thick patch of plants near the chimney. From there, I had a clear view of the opening, but I stayed hidden so nothing could see me.

***

If there's any mercy in the world, I hope someday I can forget what I saw and spend my final years in peace.

Now, I can't sleep at night unless I take medicine—and when it storms, I need something even stronger. The thing appeared suddenly, with no warning. I heard fast, rat-like scratching, like it came from deep, far-off pits I couldn't imagine. There was heavy breathing and grunts, and then, from under the chimney, something horrible burst out—an overwhelming wave of disgusting, living filth. It poured from the hole like a nightmare come to life, bubbling and oozing like the slime of snakes, spreading through the cellar and out into the dark forest, bringing fear, madness, and death with it.

I don't know how many there were—maybe thousands. Seeing them in the brief flashes of lightning was terrifying. When they started to spread out, I could make out their shapes. They were small, twisted, hairy monsters—like awful, warped versions of apes. They were terrifyingly quiet. I barely heard a sound when one of the last creatures turned and, like it had done it a hundred times before, started to eat a weaker one. Others jumped in to finish what was left, eating hungrily. Even though I was frozen in fear and disgust, my curiosity got the better of me. When the final creature crawled up alone from that nightmare tunnel, I pulled out my gun and shot it, hiding the sound in the thunder.

I can still see it in my mind—twisting, blood-red shadows running through endless, haunted hallways beneath a purple sky lit by violent lightning. I saw monstrous forests with huge, twisted oak trees whose roots slithered through the dirt, feeding on something terrible underground. I saw tentacle-like mounds reaching up from beneath the earth, and ancient stone walls covered in poison ivy and strange fungi.

Thank goodness some instinct guided me, half-conscious, back to where people lived—to a quiet village sleeping peacefully under the stars after the storm had passed.

They were creeping shapes made of red, wild chaos.

A week later, I had recovered enough to send for a team of workers from Albany. I told them to blow up the Martense mansion and the top of Tempest Mountain with dynamite, seal off every tunnel we could find, and destroy the overgrown trees that felt like an insult to sanity just by existing. After they did all of that, I was finally able to sleep a little. But I'll never truly rest, not as long as I remember the horrible secret of the lurking fear. That thing will always haunt me—because who can say for sure that we wiped it all out? What if there are more like it hiding in the earth around the world? Knowing what I know, how can I look at a subway entrance or an old well without feeling that cold chill of fear? Why can't the doctors give me something strong enough to help me sleep—or something that truly calms me when thunder rolls in?

What I saw under the beam of my flashlight after I shot that last awful creature was so disturbing and so simple that it took me nearly a minute to understand—and when I did, I nearly lost my mind. The thing lying there was disgusting: a filthy, pale, ape-like monster with dirty, tangled fur and long yellow teeth. It was the end result of animals gone completely wrong—something twisted by years of inbreeding, isolation, and cannibalism both above and below the ground. It was everything terrifying and chaotic hiding just beyond the surface of life.

Before it died, it looked straight at me. Its eyes were strange in a way that struck a deep, awful memory. One eye was blue. The other was brown. Just like in the old stories—they were the mismatched eyes of the Martense family. And in that moment of silent horror, I finally understood what had become of that vanished, thunder-maddened family.

Thank You for Reading

Dear Reader,

We hope this timeless classic has sparked your imagination and enriched your literary journey. Now that you've turned the final page, we want to share a vision for the future of reading—one where every classic you've ever wanted to explore is at your fingertips, in a format that best suits your life.

We'd like to invite you to gain immediate, unlimited digital & audiobook access to hundreds of the most treasured literary classics ever written—along with the option to secure deluxe paperback, hardcover & box set editions at printing cost. Together, we can spark a new global literary renaissance alongside our small, independent publishing house called "The Library of Alexandria."

Thousands of years ago, the Library of Alexandria stood as a beacon of knowledge—until it was lost to history. We aim to reignite that spirit of preservation and discovery right now, in the modern age—only this time, it's accessible to all, in every language and every format.

Picture a world where every timeless classic, novel, poem, or philosophical treatise is not only available to read but also updated for today's readers—modernized, translated into any language or dialect, and ready to enjoy in any format you choose, whether that is in an eBook, audiobook, paperback, or deluxe hardcover & box set version a printing cost.

By joining our movement to rebuild the modern Library of Alexandria, you become part of an unprecedented mission to offer:

- **Unlimited Audiobook & eBook Access to the Greatest Classics of All Time**

  Instantly explore thousands of legendary works, from Plato and Shakespeare to Jane Austen and Leo Tolstoy. All are instantly ready to read or listen to, giving you a complete literary universe at your fingertips.

- **Paperback & Deluxe Editions at Printing Costs:**

  Purchase any title in a paperback, deluxe hardbound, or deluxe boxset edition at printing costs, shipped right to your doorstep. Curate your personal library of Alexandria with editions worthy of display—crafted to last, designed to captivate, and delivered straight to your door.

- **Modern translations for Contemporary Readers in all languages and dialects**

  Discover a vast selection of classics reimagined in clear, current language—no more struggling with outdated phrases or obscure references. Next to the original versions, we aim to offer translations in as many languages and dialects as possible.

  As we continue our translation efforts and add new languages, readers everywhere can connect with these works as if they were written today. By bridging linguistic divides, you're contributing to ensuring that these timeless stories become more meaningful, accessible, and inspiring for people across the globe.

- **Your Personal Library of Alexandria:**

  Over the months and years, you'll curate a unique physical archive of classics—each volume a testament to your taste, curiosity, and love of knowledge. It's not just about owning books—it's about curating a cultural legacy you'll cherish and pass down for generations to come.

- **Join a Global Literary Renaissance:**

  Your support fuels an ongoing mission: allowing us to reinvest in offering deluxe print editions (including special boxsets) at their true cost, broaden the range of available formats and translations, and extend the reach of these works to new audiences worldwide. By joining today, you're not just preserving a legacy of masterpieces; you set in motion a powerful wave of literary accessibility.

We are more than a publisher—we're a movement, and we can't do it alone. Your support lets us scale our mission, preserving and reimagining history's greatest works for tomorrow's readers.

Become a Torchbearer of knowledge.

Thank you for picking up this book and allowing us into your literary journey. As you turn the pages, know that you're part of something larger: a global effort to keep these stories alive, share their wisdom across borders and generations, and spark a true cultural revival for the modern era.

If this resonates with you—please consider taking the next step by visiting:

www.libraryofalexandria.com

With gratitude and a shared love of knowledge,

The Modern Library of Alexandria Team

www.ingramcontent.com/pod-product-compliance
Lightning Source LLC
Chambersburg PA
CBHW010356310726
48979CB00006B/1055